Open the Dark

Open the Dark

poems

❧

Marie Tozier

borealbooks

Book layout by Bryan Wong

Library of Congress Cataloging-in-Publication Data

Names: Tozier, Marie, author.
Title: Open the dark : poems / Marie Tozier.
Description: First edition. | [Pasadena] : Boreal Books, [2020]
Identifiers: LCCN 2020010366 (print) | LCCN 2020010367 (ebook) | ISBN
    9781597099202 (trade paperback) | ISBN 9781597099486 (ebook)
Subjects: LCGFT: Poetry.
Classification: LCC PS3620.O988 O64 2020 (print) | LCC PS3620.O988
    (ebook) | DDC 811/.6—dc23
LC record available at https://lccn.loc.gov/2020010366
LC ebook record available at https://lccn.loc.gov/2020010367

The National Endowment for the Arts, the Los Angeles County Arts Commission, the Ahmanson Foundation, the Dwight Stuart Youth Fund, the Max Factor Family Foundation, the Pasadena Tournament of Roses Foundation, the Pasadena Arts & Culture Commission and the City of Pasadena Cultural Affairs Division, the City of Los Angeles Department of Cultural Affairs, the Audrey & Sydney Irmas Charitable Foundation, the Kinder Morgan Foundation, the Meta & George Rosenberg Foundation, the Albert and Elaine Borchard Foundation, the Adams Family Foundation, the Riordan Foundation, Amazon Literary Partnership, and the Mara W. Breech Foundation partially support Red Hen Press.

First Edition
Published by Boreal Books
an imprint of Red Hen Press
www.borealbooks.org
www.redhen.org

Acknowledgments

I would like to thank the following publications in which some of these poems first appeared:

Alaska Quarterly Review, "Approaching Winter"; *Catamaran,* "She Loved Words"; *Cirque,* "Facebook: Alaska Mystery Pictures, Investigating Unknown People"; and *Yellow Medicine Review,* "In August" and "I Woke Up."

Special thanks to Peggy Shumaker for bringing my work forward; to Kevin Goodan for thoughtful critique; to Joeth Zucco, Natasha McClellan, Rebeccah Sanhueza, and Tobi Harper of Red Hen Press, for providing extra care and effort with me and my book; to Tok and our children for the unending inspiration and love; and to my granddaughter Ahnie for the perfect quote and introduction to this book, "These are my people."

For Tok

Contents

I

II

III

Open the Dark

I

Grandmother's Bible

Grandmother had a King James Bible.
In its front pages, she had written
Each of our names and birthdates.
      She ran her hand
Down the list of deaths and showed me
Where to find our Eskimo names.

The list, in Iñupiaq, of who we were named
After. Eskimo names given
      To remember
Dear friends, siblings lost too young, esteemed
Elders. There is no why.
Only who.

Lingonberries

Creep above
Autumnal tundra

Bright red kernels
Tart on the tongue—

When fully ripe
Of burnt claret.

Approaching Winter

A lone gull makes its way
Across an expanse of silt:
Stinking of malukchuks and rotting willows,
Loose feathers and one discarded sock, which clings
To the anchor line of a dogged fisherman's net.
An abandoned snowmachine
Sunk last spring, sits exposed near the far shore.

The gull is white and mottled gray
Ambling on pink legs, long pale-yellow beak
Raised in the air; a debutante,
Unsure of how to hike her ruffled gown.

King Crab

Mighty crustacean
Of the Arctic sea
Baited into waiting pot,
And raised
From beneath thick ice
Only to be lowered in a boiling bath
And steamed
To bright perfection.
Do you feel pain?
Does it even matter?
Know that I will savor
The edible parts of you:
Your thick leg meat,
The portion hidden
In the tip of your claw
—If I were my grandmother,
The last sound would be
A long slurp as I drink and swallow
Broth from your shell.

Grandfather Says

When I was thirteen, my brothers
brought me to the ocean's still, icy
coast to teach me how to hunt seal.

My chore: to make the oatmeal
every morning. I had seen my mama
do it many times. I knew to heat

the water, to add a pinch of salt.
To add the oats and stir them
until they were done cooking.

When my brothers were ready to eat
they came, and one by one tasted
the oatmeal. They spit it out. I

tried some and spit it out.
My brothers laughed.
They never scolded,

That wasn't our way.
Salt water from the ocean.
Mama didn't tell me that.

Indian Health Services

Through the door
The cold, white-painted
Room makes me shiver.
I notice metal utensils and think
How out of place they seem.
A black nurse enters,
Asks me if I am safe
At home. "Yes," I reply.
And then, as if
My mother hadn't died
Of undiagnosed cancer, as if
The last doctor hadn't disbelieved
That I could have a blond-haired
Child, as if I weren't afraid
To keep this appointment, unwilling
To hear, *Come back in a week,*
She asks,

      Are you respected?

When Harvest Moon Lights the Sky

Between cabin and ocean lies a field.
In August, it comes alive with secrets.
Under tall grass, among the coltsfoot
And odd Jacob's Ladder: tiny red berries.
Heavy with honey-juice, they droop
And bleed. At night voles come,
To run and dig and breed,
                    In the field.

For Bert Karmun

You snapped a photo, a self-portrait

Your face framed in an old mirror

Hanging on the wall.

You surrounded yourself

With photos of family—

    Your parents

    All twelve of your siblings,

    Their children—

And other pictures you'd taken:

Mountains, a field of flowers,

Daisies with yellow button centers

    Standing at attention

On an open slope of road—

Your reflection remains

Trapped in beveled wood, mirror

Hanging on the wall.

Aakuaksrak

One spring, sandhill cranes flew into sight.
Having landed, they became hard to spot,
Their bodies and wings dirt-brown,
The color of dead willow leaves.
That fall, the crane wife fed her husband
Cranberries. He balked. He made fun
Of the tiny morsel. At night, while he slept,
She dressed his eyes in red berry pulp.
Staining him for life.

Cache

Many summers she and I worked
squatting on tundra
near the ocean, where sand
turns into beach grass, long shards
that bite the bare feet of children.

This place, her cache: the naked
tent frame, the straight poles
with their burls—skeleton
of fish rack—and the old cable wheel,
now a picnic table.

Grandmother's gone.
But we return every summer,
spawning salmon,
finding that faint
scent of home.

Abandoned

For Uncle, juvenile delinquent

Reflection
On still water

The massive
Rust-laden
Dredge

Now a seagull's
Perch. Pairs

Of white birds
Nest on

Windowsills,
Panes busted out

By teens
With nothing better to do.

My Collage

blue bird
in a paper cage
surrounded by moss-
green paint, dripping
down spackled walls
and words
fly Victoria
LOVE
scratched into
layers
of background
peeled back
and covered over
like the heart
beating again
after loss

Eli

The best camera is your mind—
Says the animated boy,
Who thinks he won't forget.

Fade

What's inside
The space
Between laughter
And the memory
Of those you laughed with?

Facebook: Alaska Mystery Pictures, Investigating Unknown People

You've seen pictures
Of long ago—
Eskimo man, his wife
Their child,

Dressed in furs
Of sealskin and reindeer

Fancy ruff outlines
A smiling face

     Dark eyes.

Illuqs looking back at you.
Your family.

They want to know

What's been lost,
What's missing.

You wear the same parka,
They whisper.

Dear ones, I say,
     It doesn't fit.

Old-Time Truck

Submerged
In a pond
Off the Nome Council Highway,
Rust-colored—
Time eating away
At the body.
A backdrop each year
For pairs of loons,
     Performing.
All that remains now
A faint memory,
A story,
Old man Kigrook
And his grandson,
     Lost while driving.

Life without Her

For Mother

Mismatched china
Trying to pass
   For a complete set.

Grandmother's Words

Ethel Davis Karmun, b. March 2, 1932, d. December 23, 2013

Babe: If you're out picking berries
And you spy a bear somewhere
Even way out on the tundra
Don't worry.
My mom said—raise your kuspuk,
Show the bear your ummas
And he'll turn and walk the other way.

I never tried it.
My husband always had his gun.
Once, Edith Iyatunguk went picking with us.
She decided to follow Dan up the hill,
They walked a long way.
When they came back my bucket was full.
Edith said—*I'll never follow Dan Karmun again.*

My mom died real young.
      She was a clean lady.

This was her platter. I didn't know at first
How she used it. See how old the wood is.
I thought it was to kupchuq; it's not.
It's to place food on the floor, for
Everyone to eat.

This was my mom's scraper.
She worked hard on the sealskins.
I remember sledding as a child.
We would go down the hill
On top of sealskins. Every time we went down,
The skins got softer.

It was fun to be a kid.
Now you're a mother,
Your babies are so fat, they sure like to umma.
I told your mom to nurse you kids, babe,
     But she let you have a bottle.
The last time I went to see the doctor,
I told him—I don't need a gown, I have nothing
Left to cover up—and he turned away.

II

They Tried to Teach Me History

The parents of these Indian children are ignorant,
and know nothing of the value of education.
—John S. Ward, US Indian Agent, 1886

THE
Beginning.
First steps,
Declaring
      What is.
Naming it.

                  Oogruk: bearded seal.

PARENTS
Defenders.
Teach a child
By example,
By witness.

              Grandfather said,
        When a young man comes of age, he
        Must learn to hunt.

OF
The Bible says
"And Jesse begat
David the king"
And aren't we all
The sons of Adam?
Each one.

THESE
Right here
        As if,
It was happening today . . .
Wait.
The schoolteacher
Stands up at City Hall,
Begs for money
To do her job.
Then blames the parents
When she fails.

INDIAN
Alaska Native
Hopi
Déné.
Inuk   the *real* people.

CHILDREN
Not vessels.
We fill them up
Not understanding,
What's useless
Can't be poured out.
They're drowning.

ARE
Is better than were.
My brother was lost.
And now he's gone.

IGNORANT
Ignorant's another word
For: Why
Can't you do it my way?
Less the guilt.

AND
What follows after dismissal
Is grief
Disaster
Destruction

        Brown faces on the street
        Corner, middle of winter,
        Waiting for bars to open.

KNOW
The difference between
Life and death
Is the difference
Between the truth
And a lie.
You can't
Take it back.
Not today. Not tomorrow. Forever.

NOTHING
Everything taken away.
Our land
Our ways
Our children
Gone.

          Abandoned qasgri, sod house,
          Returning to earth.

OF
Tell it to your children,
And let your children
Tell it to their children,
And their children
To the next generation.
          Remember.

THE
Definite.
Specified by circumstance
Un-needing of
Recognition
Or approval
Or equivocation.

                    I am enough.

VALUE
What is the fair price
Of happiness?
Can it even be measured?
Unacknowledged injustices
Are wounds left unhealed,
Left to fester
Warm to the touch.

OF
Songs unsung
Hang in the air
        No ears remain
To claim them.

                    Make them listen.

EDUCATION
Would it matter
If I laid out the process
For cutting seal:
Splitting the carcass
Separating the blubber
From the meat,
Which is dried
In the wind and sun,
Butterflied open
From tail to neck
Meat hung till black
Backbone hacked
Intestines braided
To be cleaned
Water run through them
Water
      To wash away
         The sin
      Of being.

III

Grandmother Told Me a Story

She said,
"Dan and I,
When we were young,
And there was only your mom,
And Lucille, Glenn, and Elsie,
We would pack them over to Edith's house.
Long time ago in Deering.
We'd play games and visit all night.
Finally, when it got too late,
Edith would make something up.
She said, 'TTGH,' and we had to guess
What it meant."

One year, before Christmas,
Gram got sick. As she lay in the hospital bed,
Unconscious, we sang hymns
For her. Friends visited. Her remaining
Children returned. She woke up.
She smiled and laughed—
She said,

Time to go home.

Picking Raspberries

The wild ones
Are ready in mid-July

Alaska's last
Best-kept secret

Small red fruits
On prickly green canes

Oh! Their sweet
Sweet smell

Calling the bees
And the spiders

And us
Into the ditches

Emerging
With sweat-kissed

Foreheads
Sticky fingers

And a bag full
Of bleeding drupelets.

For Zachary

While camping by the Nome River

This is how I remember you:
Bundled up in your blue-and-
White fleece jacket. Dimple
Happy. Your fat little hands
Held a paper cup, and inside
That paper cup,
A small snail.
You had to have him,
You had to keep him,
You had to name him,
Momo. We wrote his name
On the cup and took plenty
Of pictures. You tried to feed
Him. When it was time to leave
You placed him under a stick,
Certain he would survive
Cold and rain.

At Dusk

Coming home
From the river
Dressed in fog
     Which lingers
In the curves of the road,
High beams mute.

Through wisps
Of cloud
     An apparition,
A gull.
Undisturbed
By our passing.

She Even Used a Ruler

Grandmother left me her prized possessions.
Kuspuk patterns she used to outfit herself
and her daughters in custom-made tops.

Her patterns were cut from a windbreaker,
deep maroon and old. I've made the pattern
pieces my own, traced them onto brown paper.

She told me how the front piece flatters a woman,
even if she's fat. She showed me how to measure
the hood, how to press the fabric without an iron.

Her sharp eye drawn to minor flaws
She reminded me to be precise.
Use a ruler to be exact,
                    like her.

The 8th of October, 2014

At dark of night
the colding air
bites
    at once, unlike

the blood-red moon,
which takes fifty-nine—

fifty-nine minutes for my love

standing there
in his pajamas
and leather mocs,
    snapping pictures—

not for himself,
but my enjoyment,

    my eclipse.

Seasons

Seasons
Roll into each other

Spring's bud
Turns summer's leaf,

Ripe berries
Wait on the bush
Fall to winter.

In between

A long pause,
While the moon
Turns full—

Making Do

Grandfather watched
In springtime, as his older brothers
Gathered eggs.

Tethered to a handmade rope,
The eldest, Evans, would make his way
Down the rocky cliffs at Deering.

He gathered tern eggs,
Large, blue, and speckled,
Carefully placed in his sack.

When he was done, he'd tug
At the rope.

My grandfather, Daniel,
Was not yet ready to climb the cliffs,
His footing unsure.

Instead, he fashioned a long stick
With a fabric pocket. Reached down,
And swooped eggs from their nests.

For the Newly Elected School Board Member

From Anywhere but Here

Welcome to the ancestral land
Of my people. We
    Already know you:

Bossy white woman
    Thinks she
Owns the world

Rules the school
Wags her finger
    In our face

Preaches love
If only we'd listen.

Eli at Seven

And

how come, if the world

is spinning, we aren't

    spinning? And if we are

spinning, why don't we just

    fly off?

I think it's because the blood,

you know, the blood in our veins,

    it's spinning.

It keeps us from flying.

Pride

Front Street, Nome, Alaska

A drunk young man

Stands at the corner,

Hugging his new girlfriends.

Suddenly he throws

His middle fingers into the air

And yells after the police car

Haaaah, haaaah, yeahhhh!

Spectator Art

Black-beaked mask
Moves across
The floor
Bobbing this way
    And that way.

Dancer's arms a wingspan
Gliding as Raven does,
High above. Motioning
To the rhythm
Of the old skin drum.

His hands
Adorned with knitted gloves
Flex and point.
Swoosh and soar.

Raven plays, laughs at his friends
Calls down to them.

Ah-quak! Ah-quak!

(Brief silence.)

Then Eskimo hollers
And thunder claps
Fill the space
Where Raven danced.

Confection

All the health books say, "Sugar feeds the cancer."

My mother returned to me in a dream,
Her frail lace of lashes, the sweet
Medicinal-mother smell of her lip dew.
Her smile.

I don't know if anyone will remember
That she loved short ribs, salad with ginger
Sauce, baklava.

Baklava, so decadent
I refused to make it while she lay in her bed
Unable to garner an appetite—

I didn't bake it
      Until her fight was gone. The sweet
No longer a temptation.

Like a child with a tiny treasure,
She bragged on her gooey,
Honey-smothered pastry to Millie,
Her home nurse.

She stashed bits of delight
      Away in the freezer.

Fireweed

Petals of fuchsia

Simmer the field,

And fat bumblebees

Anchor themselves

To long woody stems,

Seduced by a hidden promise—

Man of Virtue

My grandfather takes the Bible
At its word. James 1:27—*to visit*
The fatherless and widows in their affliction.

Eighty years old, he travels
The smaller villages
To comfort those in mourning.
Speaks of grown men as orphans,
Those who need care.

He plays the accordion
And sings the old hymns
They all remember.

Our Lives Served upon a Platter

There's no sugar
For mother's milk.

Siblings

My grandfather
Tells me stories of his only sister,
Elsie. She died young,
Giving birth to a third child.
They were close. He played the accordion
And she the piano. But Elsie
Could read music. She played in the church.
This makes Grandfather love her more.
And in his way, when he tells
Of her death,
He never uses that word.
To him,
She began to disappear.

Campaign Season Comes Again

A summer spent
Outside, just like
Always: wind, sun,
Rain, earth, fish,
River, edible root.

Toward the end
Pale grass
Sprawls across
Hard tundra.

Cold weather
Pours frost
On the wind.

A late-season moth,
Wings quiet, sticks
To fresh paint.

Terror

Dark night.
Rain and wind
Accumulate
In the cold recess
Of an alley. A lone
Streetlamp
Exposes the site.
A crowd is gathering.
Every person there
      Is searching
          For a lost baby.
The rain falls
And fills the bed
Of a truck, as
Parents file by
Rummaging
Through a pile
Of babies—tossing them back
If it's not a match.

A Mother's Tale

I am covered in oil. Smell like a balm of heaven, a promise unbroken.
My origin the land, the river, the raven.

Hands to heal the broken star, the upended heart boy.
Warmth. Blood. Pulse. Electric body.

Sediment to filter the noise of life
And all its buzz,
Quiet the roots that tug at my hair, my feet.
Connection, click, click, clack on the thick ice.

I gather myself and swim the wide ocean.
I know for whom I return.

      Yellow the sun.
      Yellow the daisy.

Aerosol-fine mist released from the dust of plant bones as I walk the forest
Looking, searching for you.

Rose hips and pollination. Bee lover.

But here I am. Son of my blood. I am here
Holding you in a sphere of hope.

Ptarmigan mother call out to me now, show me the way from your willow
branch.
Crow overhead, sing whiskey. Sing blood. Let go your secret, your berries,
your eyelashes.
Your hand.

You looked down and I followed the moss trail, edged with wolfsbane and
at the end a light,
A shadow. Orion.

Under the sung-out tree, beside the creek he sat. Cold. Wrapped in a bear
rug, trembling.

Little Brother

We played once, at the shore

A flock of gulls
Littered the coastline.
When I find myself
Missing you, I
Return to that scene.

Pink, knobby knees
Carried by webbed feet
Play in the waves,
Which break
At the edge of ocean.

The cool water,
The breaking bubbles,
And me.

Wild Violets

Translucent petals
Grace
Bite-sized flowers
That bloom
In early summer.

In the sun, they feel
Lighter than lilac.

The fragile blossom
Quick to shrivel
Eager to drop—
Or plucked
      And eaten.

Marriage

Tok and I spend Saturday mornings making donuts.

I mix the sourdough by hand
then roll it out in portions
because we've quadrupled the recipe.

That could be defined as a Tozier thing—
wanting there to be enough for everyone.

Tok fries them, patient as the oil heats, then quick
with the batches until we're done, each donut
a golden ring.

Biographical Note

Marie Tozier is an Inupiaq poet whose work has been published in the *Cirque* and *Yellow Medicine Review*. She is an instructor for UAF Northwest Campus and has taught sewing, quilting, knitting and *qiviut* processing, and writing classes. She is also a contributor to the *Anchorage Daily News*. During her low-residency MFA at the University of Alaska, Anchorage, Tozier focused on identity in poetry. As a staff member at the University of Alaska Fairbanks, she took part in the Robert Wood Johnson Global Solutions Partnership, which allowed Tozier to visit Aotearoa (New Zealand) and learn about Māori education and culture. She also appeared on an episode of the US version of *Who Wants To Be a Millionaire?* in October 2000. She was the first Alaskan contestant to make it past the "Fastest Finger First" round and to play in the hot seat. Tozier lives in Nome, Alaska, with her husband and children.